Amelia Bedelia

Wraps It Up

Greenwillow Books, *An Imprint of HarperCollins Publishers*

Amelia Bedelia

Wraps It Up

by Herman Parish 🎁 pictures by Lynne Avril

Library of Congress Control Number: 2020942167
ISBN 978-0-06-296204-1 (hardback)—ISBN 978-0-06-296203-4 (paperback)

20 21 22 23 24 PC/BRR 10 9 8 7 6 5 4 3 2 1

 Greenwillow Books

For Gilda & Stan

Thanks for wrapping up

Christmas over the years—H. P.

With love for Jeff and Dr Walend,

who helped me wrap it up!—L. A.

Amelia Bedelia

Finally

Joy

Clay

Heather

Cliff

Wade

Dawn

Angel

Penny

Skip

Contents

Amelia
Bedelia
Wraps It
Up

Ghosts of
Christmases Past

"*A*hhhhh-*CHOO!*"

"Bless you, Amelia Bedelia!" said her father.

"My poor pumpkin," said her mother. "Are you catching a cold?"

Amelia Bedelia was holding a stack of dusty boxes. "Nope," she said. "My hands are full. I can't catch anything."

Amelia Bedelia and her parents were in the attic getting the Christmas decorations. After five trips up and down the stairs, they began opening the boxes. There were multicolored lights, long sparkly garlands, delicate glass ornaments wrapped in tissue paper, and three bright red stockings with their names embroidered on the white trim.

Amelia Bedelia looked at her dog napping on the rug in front of the tree. "Shouldn't Finally have a stocking?" she asked.

"We'll get one for you, Finally," said Amelia Bedelia's mother. "Maybe Santa will fill it with chew toys!"

"What do you want for Christmas?" Amelia Bedelia asked her parents.

Her parents smiled. "All we want for Christmas is for us to be together," said her mother.

"Family hug!" announced her father.

As Amelia Bedelia hugged her parents, she sighed. She loved her mom and dad, but sometimes they were not very helpful.

"Time to trim the tree!" said Amelia Bedelia's father.

"Goody," said her mother. "Trimming the tree is my favorite part." Amelia Bedelia looked at the tree in its stand near the front window. "Does it need to be shorter?" she asked.

"Oh, I didn't think about that," said her father. "Is the top scratching the ceiling?"

"Daddy, it's perfect!" said Amelia Bedelia.

"I picked up trimmings at that flea market last week," said Amelia Bedelia's mother. "I can't wait to put them on. They're antiques!"

"You're going to stick old flea-bitten branches on our new tree?" said Amelia Bedelia. "It's so pretty just the way it is."

"Our tree is the perfect size," agreed her mother. "But it could use a few decorations."

Amelia Bedelia's father put on some Christmas music. They all sang along as they untangled the lights and strung them on the tree.

"I'm dreaming of a white Christmas," Amelia Bedelia's father sang.

"Oh, if only we'd have a white Christmas," her mother said wistfully.

"No, thanks," said her father. "Way too much work."

Amelia Bedelia looked at the twinkling lights and the boxes of decorations, so colorful and bright. *Why would anyone want a white Christmas?* she wondered. *This is so much prettier!*

"Remind me to get tickets to the Holiday Pageant," said her mother. "It's so much fun when we all count down together before the mayor lights the tree."

"That tree is so tall, you can tell

they've never trimmed it!" said Amelia Bedelia. "Every year they need a ladder to decorate it."

The Holiday Pageant was held every Christmas Eve. The tree-lighting ceremony was followed by a concert of holiday music. Then everyone gathered for cookies and hot chocolate while Santa handed out candy canes. It was a beloved tradition in Amelia Bedelia's town.

"I can't wait to go ice skating," said Amelia Bedelia as she carefully placed a crystal icicle on the tree. "The pond froze over already."

"Great idea," said her father. "Let's go caroling too. This music is getting me in the spirit!"

"With Mom's two friends named Carol?" asked Amelia Bedelia.

"That sounds wonderful. I haven't seen Carol A. and Carol M. in a long time!" said Amelia Bedelia's mother.

Amelia Bedelia lifted the lid of a box and discovered dozens more ornaments nestled inside. She unwrapped one and held it up. It was a shiny red glass ball with BABY'S FIRST CHRISTMAS painted on it.

Her mother smiled, but her eyes brimmed with tears. "Remember?" she said to her husband. "We gave Amelia Bedelia a teddy bear twice as big as she was!"

Amelia Bedelia's father laughed. "That's right," he said. And do you remember *our* first Christmas? We were so poor we didn't have two pennies to rub together."

"Wow," said Amelia Bedelia. "You didn't even have two cents? Why did you want to rub them together? Does that bring good luck?"

"It did for us," said her mother, lost in the memory. "We made all our ornaments out of glitter and cardboard. They were so cute! When we moved, they got lost in the shuffle."

"No wonder," said Amelia Bedelia. "You shouldn't have been playing cards while you were moving."

"Hey," said Amelia Bedelia's father. "Remember we could only buy one gift for the both of us?"

"But you didn't even have two

pennies," said Amelia Bedelia. "Did the gift cost one cent?"

Her mother laughed. "We were trying not to spend *any* money, but we found this wonderful snow globe."

"A snow globe is *my* idea of a white Christmas," said her father. "The flurry only lasts for a few seconds and I don't have to shovel anything."

"We just *had* to have it," said Amelia Bedelia's mother. "There was a couple inside it that looked just like us."

"How come I've never seen this snow globe?" said Amelia Bedelia. "Did it get lost in another shuffle?"

Her parents looked at each other and laughed.

"Oh no," said her mother. "What happened was . . ."

"Uncle Marvin broke it!" her parents said together.

Amelia Bedelia had just hung a painted penguin on the tree. Now she turned around to listen. She had memorized most of her parents' stories, but this was a new one. "Tell me more!" she said.

Her father shook his head slowly. "Poor Uncle Marvin. He was walking into the living room, carrying a tray of eggnog for everyone—"

"And Daddy was under the tree, watering it," said her mother. "Uncle Marvin didn't see your dad and tripped over his legs. He fell into the tree and knocked it over. Since our ornaments were cardboard, none of them broke. But the tree toppled onto the mantel and knocked off our snow globe. It smashed into a million pieces."

"At least a million," said Amelia Bedelia's father, shaking his head. "There was glitter, glass, and eggnog everywhere. What a mess! Luckily no one was hurt."

Her mother nodded. "Poor Uncle Marvin felt terrible. He tried for years to replace our snow globe, but he never found another one just like it."

"That's really sad," said Amelia Bedelia. But inside, she was jumping for joy. Now she knew exactly what to get

her parents for Christmas this year. She
was going to find them the perfect snow
globe!

Rap for a Wrapper

"Good morning, Mr. Jack!" Amelia Bedelia sang out the next day

Mr. Jack, the school custodian, held the front door open for her. "Good morning to you, Amelia Bedelia. Look at the roses in your cheeks!" he said.

Amelia Bedelia's mittened hands flew

to her chilly cheeks. "I don't hav[...]
my cheeks," she said.

"You sure do," said Mr. Jack. "B[...]
ones!"

"On my cheeks?" said Amelia Bedelia.
"Growing?"

"Blooming like it's a summer day," said
Mr. Jack. "Brrr. Now hurry inside."

The building felt warm and cozy
after her walk to school. Amelia Bedelia
took off her hat and unwrapped her
scarf as she raced down the hallway.
She rushed into the bathroom and
looked in the mirror. Nope. No roses.
But her cheeks were certainly rosy
from the cold.

As she passed the teachers' lounge,

she heard a loud *POP!* followed by a gasp and giggles. Curious, she peered through the doorway. Angel and Dawn were sitting on the couch, surrounded by streamers and other party decorations. They were blowing up balloons.

"Amelia Bedelia!" said Angel. "Did that mean balloon scare you? I jumped three feet in the air when it popped!"

Amelia Bedelia was impressed. "Three feet? Wow." She looked around the room. "What are you guys doing?"

"It's Mrs. Hotchkiss's birthday," said Dawn. "The teachers are throwing a party for her after school. We volunteered to decorate. Want to help?"

"Sure!" said Amelia Bedelia.

The girls blew up more balloons, hung streamers and a HAPPY BIRTHDAY banner, and covered the table with a colorful cloth. Then they tossed sparkly confetti all over it.

"It looks great!" said Amelia Bedelia.

"Give me five," said Dawn, holding up her hand.

"Five what?" asked Amelia Bedelia.

"Five!" said Angel, holding up her hand.

"Like this," said Dawn, reaching up and slapping Angel's hand.

"Why didn't you just say so," said Amelia Bedelia, slapping both girls' hands. "Now give me ten!"

When the bell rang, Amelia Bedelia and her friends ran to class. They got to their classroom just as their teacher, Mrs. Shauk, was taking attendance. She handed the slip to Amelia Bedelia, whose classroom job was Message Deliverer.

Amelia Bedelia skipped down the hallway to the office and gave the attendance form to Mrs. Roman.

"How are you today, Mrs. Roman?" she asked.

Mrs. Roman looked up, startled. Amelia Bedelia was surprised to see the principal's assistant looking so frazzled.

"There's so much to do, and I still haven't wrapped Mrs. Hotchkiss's present," Mrs. Roman said. "I don't even have paper or ribbon. I've got a lot on my plate today."

Amelia Bedelia looked at the fancy plate on Mrs. Roman's desk. There was nothing on the plate at all.

"It's empty," Amelia Bedelia said.

"What's empty?" asked Mrs. Roman.

"Your plate," said Amelia Bedelia, pointing at it.

"This isn't my plate," said Mrs. Roman. "This is a birthday present for Mrs. Hotchkiss. We all chipped in."

Amelia Bedelia looked closer. "Where's the plate chipped?" she asked.

"Chipped?" cried Mrs. Roman, examining the plate. "No, no, it's fine. Don't scare me like that."

"Where's *your* plate?" Amelia Bedelia asked.

Mrs. Roman looked puzzled. "There's only one plate. This one. And I need to wrap it. Where will I find the time?"

Amelia Bedelia smiled. "Well, I can help you with both things," she said. "First of all, you can find the time on the clock behind you. Second of all, I would be happy to wrap that plate."

A look of utter relief came over Mrs. Roman's face. "Why, thank you, Amelia Bedelia!" She placed the fancy plate in a box and handed it to Amelia Bedelia, giving her permission to go to the art room during recess and wrap it.

"Hello, Amelia Bedelia," said Mr. Forest, the art teacher, when Amelia Bedelia skipped into his classroom at recess. "May I help you?"

Amelia Bedelia explained her mission.

"Gee, I don't have wrapping paper," Mr. Forest said. "But you are welcome to use any of my art supplies to do something special for Mrs. Hotchkiss."

"I know she likes hot chocolate and riding her bike," said Amelia Bedelia.

Mr. Forest nodded and said, "Her favorite flowers are daisies."

"Mine too!" said Amelia Bedelia. Daisy was also one of her best friends.

"As I recall," continued Mr. Forest, "Mrs. Hotchkiss told me that when she was a girl, she had a white rabbit named Daisy." He looked at his watch. "Time to run to a meeting. Have fun, be creative, and don't forget to—"

"Tidy up!" said Amelia Bedelia. "I won't forget. Thanks, Mr. Forest. And don't you forget—no running in the halls!"

A rabbit named Daisy, thought Amelia Bedelia. She stared at the art supplies.

"I've got it!" she cried. She grabbed a piece of white paper, a few buttons, pom-poms, tissue paper, scissors, pipe cleaners, a roll of tape, and some paste. Then she got to work.

She cut and she taped. She twisted

and she pasted. When she finished, she admired her creation. It was perfect.

When recess was over, Amelia Bedelia got back to her classroom just as her friends took their seats. She burst in, holding the package behind her back.

"Show us!" cried Holly.

"Let's see it!" shouted Pat.

"Settle down," said Mrs. Shauk.

Amelia Bedelia showed everyone the gift. It was wrapped in plain white paper with a pink pom-pom nose, white and pink tissue-paper ears, button eyes, and pipe-cleaner whiskers. A paper daisy perched over one ear. She had wrapped the plate to look like

Mrs. Hotchkiss's pet rabbit, Daisy.

The class erupted into *ooh*s and *ahh*s.

"Amazing," said Heather.

"As cute as a bug's ear," said Mrs. Shauk.

"Umm . . . thanks, I guess?" said Amelia Bedelia. She wondered if bugs had ears. If they did, could they really be cute?

"You're a great wrapper!" added Cliff.

Amelia Bedelia shook her head. "I don't know how to rap at all," she said. "Clay is the rapper!"

"Yay for Clay!" said Holly. "He makes up rhymes at the drop of a hat."

Clay grinned, tossing his cap onto the ground as he began his poem.

Meet our Amelia,

As in Bedelia.

A talented Ms., who is what is.

A wrapping whiz who knows her biz.

If you've got a present, she's got the gift

Guaranteed to give your spirits a lift.

Wrapping with flair

Extraordinaire!

Just beware—

With a talent so apparent,

Amelia Bedelia,

We hope no one steals ya!

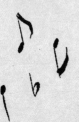

The class burst into applause. Clay took a deep bow.

"And that's a wrap," said Mrs. Shauk. "Now if you'll all open your notebooks to a clean page, we can get started."

That was *a rap*, thought Amelia Bedelia. *And a really good one too!*

New Math / Old Problem

The next day, Amelia Bedelia had an important question for her friends as they headed out for recess. "So, has everyone finished making their holiday lists?"

So far, her wish list included a scooter, rainbow socks with toes, a unicorn onesie, and a portable karaoke machine.

"I made my Hanukkah list," said Penny. "It has eight things on it."

"Mine too," said Wade. "One for every night of Hanukkah."

Penny explained, "On each night, we light the candles on the menorah, and then we open a gift," she said. "One candle on the first night, two candles on the second night, up to eight. Plus the shammash."

"What's the shammash?" asked Skip.

"That's what they call the special ninth candle in the menorah. It's usually in the middle and used to light all the other candles," said Joy.

"It's cool to get eight gifts," said Pat. "I know I want a hamster and a pogo stick. But I haven't made my whole list yet."

"I finally figured out what to get my parents," said Amelia Bedelia. "A snow globe!" She told her friends the story of Uncle Marvin and her parents' first Christmas.

"I love snow globes," said Angel. "But a good one is hard to find. You better start looking now."

"Mom, I'm home!" Amelia Bedelia called. Slipping off her backpack, she raced upstairs to her bedroom. She knew Angel was right. It could take a while to find the perfect snow globe.

For starters, she stood on her tiptoes to reach her piggy bank on the top shelf of her closet. A good shake made the coins rattle. *So far, so good,* she thought as she sat down. She pulled out the cork, spilling her savings onto the rug. To her dismay, she counted only $3.47.

"Uh-oh," she said to Finally, who had followed her up the stairs. "I forgot that I spent my allowance already." Finally looked at her quizzically. "Remember?" Amelia Bedelia said. "I bought all those comics and those glow-in-the-dark shoelaces."

Finally wagged her tail, as if to say, *Well, you really did need those shoelaces.*

Amelia Bedelia nodded. "Thank you, Finally."

She picked up two pennies and rubbed them together. At least things weren't as bad as her parents' first Christmas!

Amelia Bedelia put all the coins back in her piggy bank. Then she sat down to do her homework. Her final math problem gave her an idea. "Lucy gets $6.50 a week in allowance," she read out loud.

Hmmm, she thought. *Lucy makes way more than I do.* She kept reading. "If Lucy buys a chocolate bar for $2.50, a pack of gum for $1.65, and a lollipop for ninety-five cents, how much of her allowance is left?"

Amelia Bedelia added and subtracted. She came up with the answer, checked it, and closed her notebook with a bang. She bounded down the stairs and went straight to the kitchen. Her father stood at the counter, peeling carrots.

"Hi, Daddy," said Amelia Bedelia, getting straight to work. She picked the place mats up off the counter and arranged them on the table. Then she opened the cupboard and grabbed the plates.

"Am I seeing things?" her father said with a laugh.

"I don't know," said Amelia Bedelia. "What do you see?"

"A very helpful daughter setting the table without being asked," he replied. "What's going on?"

"Well, now that you mention it," said Amelia Bedelia, "I was wondering if I could increase my allowance by adding more chores."

Just then her mother walked in and

grabbed a carrot off the cutting board. She smiled at Amelia Bedelia. "That's my girl!"

"Sounds good," said Amelia Bedelia's father. "Let's come up with some ideas."

They all made suggestions. Soon they had a new chore list. Also, a new and improved allowance of $6.50 a week.

☑ Make bed

☑ Take Finally for a walk after school*

☑ Set dinner table

☑ Clear dinner table

☑ Load dishwasher

☑ Unload dishwasher*

(*New chores)

Amelia Bedelia nodded. "Okay. I just have one more question." Her parents stared back at her. Amelia Bedelia took a deep breath and said, "Can I get my new allowance right away? Like maybe a month's worth?" She had done some quick calculations in her head and figured that the new amount plus the $3.47 in her piggy bank would be enough to buy a very nice snow globe.

"Why, are you broke?" asked her father.

"I don't think so," said Amelia Bedelia, looking at both of her legs and each of her arms. "Do I look busted?"

"Not at all, sweetie," said her mother. "We are relieved you're in one piece."

"Me too," said Amelia Bedelia.

Her parents were glancing at each other and arching their eyebrows up and down. This was how they spoke to each other in the secret language of parents. Her mother continued, "But it's important to earn your allowance each week. So, no advances."

"Money doesn't grow on trees," said her father.

Amelia Bedelia was thinking how wonderful a money tree would be, when her mother turned to her father. "Speaking of trees," she said. "Did you put up our outdoor lights yet?"

Amelia Bedelia's father groaned. "Not yet," he said. "It takes so long, and it's freezing out there!"

Her mother sighed. "I'm not one to talk. I haven't even started addressing our holiday cards yet."

"Two very thankless jobs," her father said.

"Don't worry," said Amelia Bedelia. "I'll thank both of you!"

Amelia Bedelia's mother smiled. "That's very thoughtful, sweetie," she said. "But it doesn't make those jobs any easier."

After dinner, Amelia Bedelia cleared the table and loaded the dishwasher. Then she headed upstairs and re-counted the money in her piggy bank. Unfortunately, nothing had changed. She still had $3.47. At the rate she was going, it would be the

new year before she had enough money
to buy the snow globe. And that would
be way too late. Amelia Bedelia decided
that she would love to trim a few dollars
off a money tree.

All Ears

Amelia Bedelia plopped down at the lunch table, right across from Holly and Heather. She glanced at them, then did a double take. Both girls were wearing funny green hats with large pointy ears attached to them. Amelia Bedelia opened her mouth to say something, then closed it.

"Did you want to say something, Amelia Bedelia?" Holly asked.

"We're all ears," said Heather with a giggle.

Holly started to laugh. She pulled on her ears and stuck out her tongue at Heather, who started to laugh so hard she had to spit out her milk.

Amelia Bedelia started to laugh too. She couldn't help it. "Not completely . . . but your ears *are* enormous," she said. "Why are you wearing those silly hats?"

"They're part of our costume for the Holiday Pageant," explained Holly. "Ms. Raphael wants to try something different this year. Along with music, we're also going to do a play called 'A Visit to

Santa's Workshop.' Heather and I are elves. Aren't these hats so cute? Ms. Raphael said we could wear them to get into the holiday spirit. She accidentally ordered too many."

"Very cute," said Amelia Bedelia. "And very pointy." She opened her lunch bag and took out her lunch. She sighed.

"What's wrong, Amelia Bedelia? Don't you like your food today?" asked Cliff. "Do you want to swap cookies? I made these myself."

"Thanks, but that's not it," said Amelia Bedelia. "I'm just disappointed that I can't buy the Christmas gift I want for my parents."

"How come?" asked Heather.

"Are you short?" Clay asked.

"No, I'm tall for my age," said Amelia Bedelia.

"You may have inches, but do you have dollars?" asked Clay.

"I only have $3.47," said Amelia Bedelia, nibbling on her sandwich. "That's the problem."

"You make great lemon tarts," said Angel softly. "Maybe you could sell some."

"Then you'd have some dough!" said Clay. He laughed and slapped the table.

"But I can't even make dough if I can't afford the ingredients," said Amelia Bedelia.

"You're an expert at wrapping presents," said Wade. "Start a business wrapping people's holiday gifts!"

Amelia Bedelia perked up instantly. "That's a great idea!" she said. "I could put up signs in town and hand them out to shoppers." She felt very excited. She'd be helping people cross something off their holiday to-do lists *and* making money to buy a snow globe for her parents.

"Can I help you?" asked Dawn. "I really want to get my grandma a jewelry box this year."

"Sure! Thanks!" said Amelia Bedelia. "Together we'll get twice as much wrapping done!"

The rest of her friends joined in. "Me too! Me too! I want to help!"

Amelia Bedelia was happy her friends

wanted to help her. But she was also getting a bit worried. Would she be able to make enough money for a snow globe if she had to share her earnings with so many helpers?

"I'm no good at wrapping," Cliff confessed. "What else I could do? Make some holiday cookies?"

"That is the best idea ever!" said Amelia Bedelia. "We won't just wrap gifts, we can help out with all sorts of holiday chores! Everyone can have a different job!"

"I'm good at drawing," said Clay. "Can I help Cliff decorate cookies?"

"Definitely!" Cliff said.

Holly put her arm around Heather.

"We could go caroling at holiday parties," she said.

"Oh, do you know the Carols too?" asked Amelia Bedelia.

"We know lots of carols," said Holly.

"How many?" asked Amelia Bedelia. "My mom knows two."

"I know dozens," said Heather.

"Wow," said Amelia Bedelia. She was impressed.

"I love 'Jingle Bells,'" said Holly.

"Me too!" said Heather.

Angel and Dawn volunteered to hang holiday lights.

Wade and Daisy offered to string popcorn-and-cranberry garlands for Christmas trees.

Penny opened her notebook and started writing down everyone's ideas. She sighed. "I wish there was something I could do," she said.

Amelia Bedelia looked at the list. Then she smiled. "Penny, you have the neatest handwriting of all. Do you want to address holiday cards?"

Penny grinned. "Yup. That's the perfect job for me!" she said.

"Then it's all settled," said Amelia Bedelia. "Each of us has a holiday task. There's just one more thing. What should we call ourselves?"

"How about Holiday Helpers?" said Dawn.

"Ho-Ho-Helpers!" said Daisy.

48

"Red-Nosed Reindeers," sang Holly and Heather in perfect harmony.

Amelia Bedelia stared at Holly and Heather. "Can you borrow more of those goofy hats with the pointy ears attached?" she asked. "Enough for all of us?"

Holly shrugged. "Sure!" she said.

Amelia Bedelia looked around the table and smiled. "How about Holiday Elfers?" she said.

The answer was a resounding cheer.

STRESSED OUT?
If your
holiday TO-DO LIST
is doing you in,
let the HOLIDAY Elfers help!
* We'll wrap your gifts,
* bake cookies,
* address cards,
* hang lights,
* entertain guests,
* even string your tree
with popcorn and cranberries!

Take an Elf Flyer

"May I elf you?" Clay said to Amelia Bedelia, bowing so deeply that his hat fell off.

Amelia Bedelia laughed so hard she dropped the garland she was holding. All the Holiday Elfers were gathered in her driveway. Daisy and Wade had each brought a wagon, and the Elfers were decorating them. These would be used to transport gifts and cookies to future customers. Right now they were filled with empty boxes that Amelia Bedelia had wrapped, as samples of her designs.

Penny picked up one of Amelia Bedelia's creations. Amelia Bedelia had wrapped one small, one medium, and one large box in plain white paper. Then she had taped them together, cutting out eyes, a mouth, a carrot nose, and a top hat from construction paper. She'd tied a piece of fabric around the "neck" for a scarf and placed a row of buttons down the front.

"I love your snowman!" Penny exclaimed.

"Thanks," said Amelia Bedelia. She was very proud of all her designs.

"Here's the flyer I made," said Clay, handing her one.

"It looks amazing!" said Amelia Bedelia. "I can't believe you did it so quickly."

"Yup. I burned the candle at both ends," he replied.

"Who knew they made two-ended candles?" said Amelia Bedelia. She read the flyer out loud to her fellow Elfers.

STRESSED OUT?
If your holiday TO-DO LIST is doing you in,
Let the HOLIDAY HELFERS help!
*We'll wrap your gifts,
*bake cookies,
*address cards,
*hang lights,
*entertain guests,
*even string your tree with popcorn and cranberries!

"Okay, sign us up!" said a voice from above. The Elfers looked up to see Amelia Bedelia's parents standing over them, their arms full of outdoor lights.

"Howdy, Holiday Elfers!" Amelia Bedelia's father said. "We'd love to be your first customers."

"Thanks, Daddy," said Amelia Bedelia. She pointed to Angel and Dawn. "Meet your light-hanging Elfers!"

The girls began untangling the lights.

"I'm warning you," said Amelia Bedelia's father. "This is a thankless job."

"That's okay," said Dawn. "It's worth it! Plus, we love Christmas lights!"

"Okay, Elfers," said Amelia Bedelia. "Let's head into town to sign up customers!"

"I'll come along for the ride," said her mother. "I'm getting Finally a Christmas stocking filled with treats."

Amelia Bedelia gave her mother a funny look. "Um, Mom, I don't think you're going to fit in our wagon," she said.

"I'll walk," said her mother.

"Me too," said Amelia Bedelia. "Onward, Elfers!"

When they got to Main Street, Amelia Bedelia's mother grabbed a flyer to post at Pet Palace. The Elfers decided that Daisy would take her wagon to the grocery store, while Wade took his to the town square. Amelia Bedelia, Holly, Heather, Penny, Cliff, and Clay each took a stack of flyers to post in the

local shops and to hand out to potential customers.

"See you at noon, in front of city hall!" Amelia Bedelia called out.

"I'll be there with bells on!" shouted Daisy.

"Oh, that will really be Christmas-y," said Amelia Bedelia. "We should all sew bells on our shoes!"

Amelia Bedelia headed to her first stop, Mrs. B's Books.

"Hi, Mrs. Borello," said Amelia Bedelia. "May I put a flyer on your door?"

"Feel free," Mrs. Borello replied.

"Okay," said Amelia Bedelia. She stared at Mrs. Borello, waiting for an answer.

"Yes, Amelia Bedelia?" Mrs. Borello said.

"Would it be okay to hang my flyer on your door?" Amelia Bedelia asked again.

"Feel free, Amelia Bedelia," said Mrs. Borello.

Amelia Bedelia smiled—she felt free and easy. But Mrs. Borello seemed a little distracted.

"It's not very big," said Amelia Bedelia. "Can I tape it up?"

"Feel free!" said Mrs. Borello. "You bet!"

Maybe the holidays are getting to her already, thought Amelia Bedelia.

"We Holiday Elfers will take away your holiday stress!" she said, taping the flyer to the door.

Rap Is in Season

$\mathcal{A}$melia Bedelia's next stop was a shop called Gift Horse. They had a fine collection of snow globes on display near the door. Amelia Bedelia picked up the globes one after another and shook each one. She was spellbound watching the white glitter swirl around inside the globes, each with a different wintry scene: a jolly Santa in a sleigh, penguins around a snowman, a red cardinal on an evergreen branch. But none of the snow globes looked like the one that her parents had described, a couple outside a cozy cottage.

"When will you get your horses in?" Amelia Bedelia asked the shopkeeper.

The shopkeeper smiled. "Oh, I didn't order any," she said. "But I am expecting some plush llamas."

"Then why is your store named Gift Horse?" asked Amelia Bedelia.

"They say you shouldn't look a gift horse in the mouth!" the shopkeeper said with a laugh.

"Why not? Do they have bad breath?"

asked Amelia Bedelia. She had given up asking for a horse for Christmas and her birthday every year. If she ever did get one, now she would be sure not to look it in the mouth.

After she had hung her flyer on the window, Amelia Bedelia headed down the block to Animal Haven, the shelter where she had adopted Finally. She knew they had a bulletin board. When she got there, the door opened and a woman strode out, led by a dog on a leash.

"Hello, Doc Wiggins," said Amelia Bedelia. Dr. Wiggins was the shelter's director.

"How nice to run into you, Amelia Bedelia!" she said.

"You almost did," said Amelia Bedelia. "Who is this?"

"An English bulldog, our latest rescue," said Doc Wiggins. "He looks tough, but he's a sweetie. What brings you here? And how is that wonderful pup of yours?"

"Finally is great," said Amelia Bedelia. "Would it be okay to put a sign on your bulletin board?" She explained her business while kneeling to scratch the bulldog's tummy.

"Sounds great! Post your flyer!" said Doc W. "Come on, boy! Keep walking." But the dog refused and stretched out on Amelia Bedelia's feet instead.

"He doesn't want to go," said Amelia Bedelia.

"He's chilly," said Doc W. "Our dogs need sweaters to keep them warm, but our budget is so tight." She sighed. "But as you know, if wishes were horses, beggars would ride."

Amelia Bedelia had never heard that, just like she didn't know about looking in the mouth of a gift horse. She was glad she'd never gotten a horse for a present, after all.

"Come along, Jack Frost," said the doc, tugging on the leash.

"That's a good name," said Amelia Bedelia.

"He was found without a tag on the day of the first frost, so we named him Jack Frost," said Dr. Wiggins. "He seems to like it." The dog slowly rose to his feet.

"It's perfect," said Amelia Bedelia. "Goodbye, Doc W. Goodbye, Jack Frost."

Amelia Bedelia went inside Animal Haven, posted a flyer, then ran to meet her fellow Elfers at city hall by noon.

"Did we sign up any customers?" asked Amelia Bedelia, when she saw her friends.

Daisy and Wade shook their heads.

"Everyone's in such a rush to do their shopping," said Dawn. "No one even stopped to take a flyer from me."

"Me neither," said Wade.

Penny sipped cocoa from a paper cup. Amelia Bedelia guessed that she had been to

Pete's Diner. Pete made the best hot cocoa in town, with extra mini marshmallows.

"Why don't we carol?" suggested Holly. "That might get everyone's attention."

Amelia Bedelia looked around. "There isn't a Carol in sight," she said.

Heather smiled. "There are always carols," she said.

She and Holly started to sing. "When the snow lay 'round about, deep and crisp and even . . ." The other Elfers joined in.

But nobody stopped . . . although someone did toss a coin into Penny's hot chocolate. *SPLOOSH!*

"It's no use," said Amelia Bedelia. "Everyone is rushing around. They are too busy being busy."

"Hey, I know what to do!" said Clay.
He jumped to the middle of the sidewalk
and tossed his hat onto the ground.

Hey holiday shoppers—and your pups.
We have a favor for you grown-ups!
You'll want to hear it,
it's the least you can do,
Cause we're savin' your season.
And here is the reason.
We're the Holiday Elfers—
that's right, Elfers—
Like Santa's crew, but we're not freezin'.
We're the Holiday Elfers!
Got a task that you dread?
Don't do it! Talk to us instead.

As you can see, we're All Ears
Give us your stress, fuss, and fears.
We're the Holiday Elfers—
your very best helpers!
Are you a
Got-too-many-presents-to-wrap yelper?
Need an
Address-all-my-Christmas-cards Elfer?
How about an
I-forgot-to-bake-cookies helper?

Best of all? Our fee is reasonable.
To beat the stress that's seasonable,
All you have to do is listen to me:
We'll wrap four gifts
for the price of three!
Take a flyer to see for yourself—

You'll save big with a Holiday Elf-er.
With a Holiday Elfer you'll save
lots of time
T-t-t-that's all folks,
that's the end of my rhyme!

Decorating
with Daisy

*I*t worked! A big crowd of shoppers gathered around and began clapping to the beat. In a flash, Amelia Bedelia and her friends began passing out flyers. Then everyone started talking at once.

"My grandma used to string popcorn and cranberries—it was my favorite decoration when I was little!" said a woman in a red parka. "But it's so much trouble. I'll sign up for that!"

"Can you perform at my Hanukkah party?" a man in a ski hat asked.

An elderly woman handed Amelia Bedelia two heavy shopping bags. "Please wrap these gifts like that adorable snowman!" she said.

"Do you have any wrapping paper with holly on it?" asked another man.

Amelia Bedelia grinned at her friend Holly. "See, you're already famous!"

Amelia Bedelia steered customers to Penny, who was frantically writing down requests. Then she arched an eyebrow and turned toward Clay. "Four gifts for the price of three, huh?" Amelia Bedelia said. "Nice job of giving away our profits."

Clay shrugged. "It was the only rhyme I could come up with," he confessed. "It's a package deal."

Amelia Bedelia frowned. "Wrapping four gifts for the price of three doesn't sound like such a great deal to me," she said.

"It is, for customers!" said Clay. "It will get the Holiday Elfers off the ground."

Amelia Bedelia laughed. Now Clay was just being silly. All they really had to do was jump.

Just then Amelia Bedelia's mother arrived with her arms full of shopping bags. A stocking with Finally's name embroidered on it poked out of the top of one of them. "Look at that line," said Amelia Bedelia's mother, scanning the crowd. "You drummed up a lot of customers!"

"We didn't have a drum," said Amelia Bedelia. "Clay did a rap!"

After the last order had been taken, the Elfers headed back to Amelia Bedelia's house, their wagons full of gifts to be wrapped.

"Think it'll snow for Christmas?" Heather asked.

"I hope so," said Wade. "It doesn't feel like Christmas without snow."

"I agree," said Amelia Bedelia's mother.

Penny caught up with Amelia Bedelia.

"Did you find a snow globe?" she whispered.

Amelia Bedelia shook her head. "Nope," she said. "Still looking."

"I'll keep my fingers crossed," said Penny.

"You better not," said Amelia Bedelia. "You have a zillion cards to address!"

When they arrived at Amelia Bedelia's house, Dawn and Angel were putting the finishing touches on the outdoor lights. While the Holiday Elfers and Amelia Bedelia's mother stood on the sidewalk, her father plugged in the lights, and the porch and the trees in front of the house lit up.

"Oooooh!" everyone gasped, then applauded.

"Great job, light-hanging Elfers," Amelia Bedelia. "Now the cookie-baking Elfers, the card-addressing Elfer, the popcorn-stringing Elfers, and the gift-wrapping Elfer have to get to work!"

"And I've got to write a rhyme for that party," said Clay.

For the next two weeks, the Holiday Elfers were as busy as, well, Santa's elves. They worked every day (once they had finished their homework) and on the weekends too. Everyone pitched in. The light-hanging Elfers helped the cookie-baking Elfers and the caroling Elfers helped the popcorn-and-cranberry-stringing Elfers, and the card-addressing Elfer helped the gift-wrapping Elfer. And vice versa.

On Saturday they met to discuss the orders for the next week. And to count their earnings.

"Since we help each other out, let's pool the money," suggested Daisy.

Amelia Bedelia wasn't sure that putting their money into a pool would help. Was wet money worth more? Plus, it was way too cold to go swimming. "Let's divide it equally so we can do our Christmas shopping," she said.

"Sounds like a plan!" said Penny.

Once the money was divided up, Amelia Bedelia discovered that she had more than enough to buy the best snow globe in town. There was just one problem—the Holiday Elfers were so busy! When was Amelia Bedelia going to find time to go shopping?

To make things worse, Amelia Bedelia was stumped. Someone wanted her to wrap gifts so they looked like trees in a magical forest.

"I hate to disappoint a customer," said Amelia Bedelia. "But I don't have a clue how to do what she wants."

Daisy, who had come over to help, sat across the table from Amelia Bedelia. "What if you wrap half the presents with tree paper and half with glittery star-patterned paper?" she suggested.

"We might as well try it," said Amelia Bedelia. She put the first gift to be wrapped on her dining-room table.

"Wait a second," said Daisy. "Something just struck me!"

"Are you okay?" asked Amelia Bedelia, looking up at the ceiling for what might have fallen on her friend.

Daisy grabbed the roll of white paper that Amelia Bedelia had used for her snowman and polar bear designs. "Let's make our own wrapping paper!" she said.

Working together, the two girls gathered two clean sponges, a pair of scissors, a couple of paper plates, and some red, green, and yellow glitter paint.

Daisy cut one sponge into a simple Christmas-tree shape. Then she cut the other into a star shape. She poured the paints onto paper plates and spread out a large piece of white paper. She dipped the tree-shaped sponge into the green glitter paint and pressed it onto the paper, then did the same with the star-shaped sponge and the yellow glitter paint. She alternated until the paper was covered with trees and stars.

"That looks great!" said Amelia Bedelia.

"Just wait!" said Daisy. When the paint was dry, she dipped her finger into

the red glitter paint. She covered one of the Christmas trees with red fingerprint ornaments.

"Perfect!" said Amelia Bedelia. "I have an idea!"

Amelia Bedelia took a tiny paintbrush and dipped it into the yellow glitter paint. Then she carefully traced a miniature star on the top of the tree that Daisy had decorated.

"Ta-dah!" said Daisy.

The two girls decorated all the trees. When they had finished, they stood back and admired their handiwork.

"Daisy, you're amazing!" Amelia Bedelia said.

"I couldn't have done it without you,"

said Daisy. "You know what they say: There is no *I* in *team*."

Amelia Bedelia nodded and said, "You would know, Daisy. You are the best speller in class!"

Mixed-Up Mistakes

Ding dong! Amelia Bedelia rang her next-door neighbor's doorbell. She was delivering Mrs. Adams's order: a plate of assorted holiday cookies and two custom-wrapped gifts: a package shaped like a polar bear, with a tag that read OONA, and another one wrapped as a penguin, with a tag that read GEORGE.

"Perfect timing, Amelia Bedelia," said Mrs. Adams. "My guests just arrived. Will you join us for tea and cookies?"

Amelia Bedelia had half a dozen more gifts to wrap, but she loved visiting Mrs. Adams, who still sometimes babysat for her. Besides, she was overdue for a cookie break.

She handed Mrs. Adams the gifts and walked into the living room. She set the plate of cookies down on the coffee table. A girl with long brown hair who looked not much older than Amelia Bedelia sat on the couch next to a gentleman with a bald head and a snow-white beard.

"Amelia Bedelia," said Mrs. Adams,

"meet my brother, George, and my grandniece, Oona."

"Hi," said Oona, giving Amelia Bedelia a little wave.

George stood and shook her hand. "Were your ears ringing?" he asked. "We were just hearing about your new business."

"Actually, I hear ringing all the time," said Amelia Bedelia. "We Holiday Elfers wear bells on our shoes to keep in the spirit of the holidays."

The kettle began whistling, so Mrs. Adams headed for the kitchen. "Will you unwrap the cookies, Amelia Bedelia?" she called back over her shoulder.

"These look amazing!" exclaimed

Oona. She took a thumbprint cookie that was filled with raspberry jam.

George helped himself to a chocolate crinkle cookie covered in powdered sugar. Amelia Bedelia took two snowman sugar cookies, one for her and one for Mrs. Adams, who had returned with her hands full. She was carrying a tray holding a pretty teapot with matching cups and saucers, a bowl of sugar cubes, and a tiny pitcher of milk. She poured everyone a cup.

"Oh, I can't wait," said Mrs. Adams. "Amelia Bedelia wrapped your gifts. Aren't they splendid? Go ahead, open them!"

She handed Oona the polar bear and George the penguin.

"What a lovely wrapping job," said George. "It's a crime to tear it!"

"I won't arrest you," said Amelia Bedelia. "Go ahead."

He began to take off the paper carefully, making sure not to crease it.

"It is super cute," said Oona. Then she tore the wrapping right off and lifted the lid on the box inside.

"Golf balls!" said Oona.

George opened his box and peered inside. "Hair chalk!" he said.

Mrs. Adams turned to Amelia Bedelia with a look of alarm on her face.

Amelia Bedelia jumped up. Oh no! She had mixed up the gift tags!

Her mind was racing to explain, but all

she could say was "I . . . I . . . I . . ."

"I'm speechless!" said George, looking at his sister.

You aren't speechless, thought Amelia Bedelia. *You just said something. I really am* speechless!

"I mean," George continued, "how did you know that I've been wanting to color my beard bright blue?"

"And that I just joined the golf team at school?" said Oona. "Thank you, Aunt Mary Jean."

Amelia Bedelia glanced at Mrs. Adams. She rolled her eyes in relief. Close call!

It was time for Amelia Bedelia to get back to work. Mrs. Adams walked her to the door. "Sorry about the gift tag mix-up!" Amelia Bedelia said.

"I'm not," said Mrs. Adams. "My brother is getting a blue beard and Oona might get a hole in one. What lucky gifts! When they use them, I'll be tickled pink!"

"That's an easy gift to give," said Amelia Bedelia. She reached out and started tickling Mrs. Adams.

"Stop, enough!" cried Mrs. Adams, laughing.

Then George and Oona joined in, and they kept tickling Mrs. Adams until the tops of her ears turned pink.

"I like giving a gift I don't have to wrap," said Amelia Bedelia. "That is your present to me."

9

Cranking Out Cookies

After Amelia Bedelia had wrapped and delivered the last of the gifts, she checked in on the rest of the Elfers to see how they were doing. She helped Angel and Dawn hang lights on the McGurks' house on President Street. She walked to the post office to mail the stack of Christmas cards that Penny had carefully addressed and stamped. Then she headed to Cliff's house. He and Clay had several large cookie orders that were due the next day, and they needed help baking and decorating.

When Amelia Bedelia arrived, Cliff was pulling three dozen Santa's whisker cookies out of the oven. She helped Cliff and Clay pack them into pretty boxes. Daisy and Penny came by with Daisy's wagon to deliver them to Mrs. West, who lived over by Pleasant Street Park. Meanwhile, Cliff began rolling out the dough for their biggest order yet—two hundred reindeer cookies for the Holiday Pageant. The cookies had to be finished by the end of the day, and they would be delivered first thing in the morning. Amelia Bedelia searched through the pile of cookie cutters for the one they needed.

"I've got some bad news," she said. "I can't find the reindeer."

"Isn't that it?" Cliff pointed to a cutter.

Amelia Bedelia held it up. "That's a horse," she said.

"Oops," said Cliff. "I thought that was a reindeer. That means we don't have one." He bit his lip. "The Baker's Dozen is the only place in town that sells cookie cutters. And they're closed today."

"Do they have to be reindeer cookies?" Clay asked.

Amelia Bedelia began sorting through the cookie cutters they did have. "How about Santa . . . or an angel . . . or a Christmas tree?" she asked.

"No dice," said Cliff.

"That's okay. I don't think we have one in the shape of dice anyway," said Amelia Bedelia. She picked up a cookie cutter. "How about a gingerbread man?"

Cliff shook his head. "The director, Ms. Raphael, specifically requested two hundred reindeer cookies," he said. "I guess I'll call her and see if we can make another kind."

Amelia Bedelia put the gingerbread man cookie cutter back down on the counter. Then she stared at it. "Wait a minute!" she said. She turned it upside down. "Doesn't this look exactly like a reindeer head?"

"I don't see it," said Cliff.

"Me neither," said Clay.

"See—the legs are the antlers, the head is the nose, and the arms are the ears!" she told them. "It's perfect!"

"You turned a gingerbread man into a reindeer?" asked Clay. "Amelia Bedelia, is there anything you can't do?"

She nodded. "Cartwheels." Then she lowered her head. "And I also can't find the perfect snow globe for my parents."

"You still have time," Cliff said.

"Maybe not. I'm worried," said Amelia Bedelia. "Christmas is two days away."

"Never say never," said Clay.

"I didn't," said Amelia Bedelia.

"Didn't what?" said Clay.

"Say you-know-what," she said.

"It's cool," said Clay. "You can make anything."

Amelia Bedelia looked at Clay. Then she looked at him again. She smiled. He was right.

"Let's get baking," said Cliff, "or we'll nev—." He caught himself before he said the forbidden word. "Once we finish baking, we'll have two hundred cookies to decorate!"

Later that evening, Amelia Bedelia's mother came to her bedroom to tuck her in. She sat on the edge of Amelia Bedelia's bed and stroked her hair.

"You really did an amazing job helping the town get ready for the holidays," she said. "I'm so proud of you and your friends for all your hard work. You made everyone's holiday better. I've got to hand it to you, peanut."

"Oh, yay! What are you handing me?" said Amelia Bedelia. "An advance on my allowance?"

Her mother smiled. "You'll have to wait until Christmas morning," she said. She stood up. "And no advances."

"Don't forget to wake me up early," Amelia Bedelia said. "We have to deliver the cookies for the pageant."

"I have to be up early too," her mother told her. "I volunteered to help out at the holiday breakfast at Shady Acres and then drive the residents to the pageant.

So I'll meet you and Daddy there." Shady Acres was a retirement village in town where Amelia Bedelia's mother often volunteered.

Amelia Bedelia's father appeared in the doorway. "Dear old Dad here with the weather report," Then he made his voice sound like an announcement from a loudspeaker. "Good chance of a light dusting of snow overnight. I repeat, good chance of a light dusting of snow tonight."

"Hope the dusting doesn't make anyone sneeze," said Amelia Bedelia.

Amelia Bedelia's father smiled at her mother. "Looks like you might be getting a White-ish Christmas after all."

"I'll take any flake I can get," said Amelia Bedelia's mother.

"Are you referring to me?" said Amelia Bedelia's father.

"Being flakey is what I love best about you," said her mother.

"I'm dreaming of a white-ish Christmas," Amelia Bedelia sang as her mother kissed her forehead and turned out the light. Everything was coming true. Her parents' snow globe. A possible white-ish Christmas. The reindeer cookies. Once they had delivered the cookies to the pageant, Christmas vacation would officially begin. Amelia Bedelia had certainly earned hers.

10

Snowbound
for Glory

"**R**ise and shine, daughter of mine," Amelia Bedelia's father called out the next morning.

Amelia Bedelia yawned and stretched. "Did we get our dusting of snow?" she asked.

Her father shook his head. "Nope."

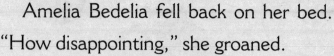

Amelia Bedelia fell back on her bed. "How disappointing," she groaned.

Her father walked over to the window and pulled up the shade. A bright white light flooded her room. Amelia Bedelia gasped. Everything was covered in a thick layer of fluffy snow. Lawns, roofs, and backyards were buried. Cars parked on her street were now white humps.

"Enough dust for you?" her father asked.

"Mom must be so happy!" said Amelia Bedelia.

"Your mom is over the moon," said her father.

Amelia Bedelia imagined her mom

riding the cow that jumped over the moon. "When is she coming back?" she asked.

"She's in the kitchen now," said Amelia Bedelia's father. "Making pancakes to celebrate."

After breakfast, Amelia Bedelia got dressed. Long johns. Wool socks. A big sweater. By the time she had stuffed herself into her snow pants, she knew how a sausage felt. She pulled on her boots, hat, and mittens, and headed outside. She leaped off the steps—and sank into snow above her knees. Luckily, Finally, who loved the snow, landed on top of her and didn't disappear entirely.

"We'll need the sled!" she yelled to her parents.

Her mother came to the door. "Sweetie, the pageant director just called. The roads are closed. The pageant has been canceled."

"Oh no!" Amelia Bedelia groaned.

Her father poked his head out the door and gave a low whistle. "My kingdom for a snowplow," he said.

Amelia Bedelia shook her head. "All those cookies!"

"What a shame," Amelia Bedelia's mother said. "The folks at Shady Acres will be crushed."

Amelia Bedelia gasped. "By an avalanche?"

A big slab of snow slid off their roof onto the front porch. Finally barked and barked.

"No, no, they're safe and sound," her mother said. "They will just be sad to miss the pageant. And I'm sad I can't take them to it."

Amelia Bedelia made a snowball and threw it at her swing set. She hit her slide with a *BONK*, sending more snow sliding down. Then she brightened up. "If you can't take them to the pageant, Mom, what if we bring the pageant to them?"

Ninety minutes and dozens of phone calls later, the Holiday Elfers had gathered in Amelia Bedelia's front yard. Some Elfers had walked over, using snowshoes. Those who lived farther away had strapped on cross-country skis for the journey. Amelia Bedelia's parents joined them, along with Finally, who was wearing a holiday sweater and a pair of reindeer antlers. The Elfers loaded the reindeer cookies onto Amelia Bedelia's sled. Amelia Bedelia put Finally on top.

"I've always wanted to drive a dogsled," said Amelia Bedelia. "Mush!"

The deep snow made for very slow going. After fifteen minutes, it was time for a break.

"Phew," said Penny. "My legs are spaghetti."

Clay laughed. "Next time we'll bring

meatballs and tomato sauce."

Amelia Bedelia knew that Clay was probably joking, but she still shuddered at the thought.

Once they had all caught their breath, they started out on their trek again.

"Jingle bells, jingle bells, jingle all the way!" Holly sang at the top of her lungs. Soon, all the Holiday Elfers joined in.

The door of a nearby house opened. A woman looked out and waved.

"Hey, there's Carol A!" Amelia Bedelia's mother called. "We're bringing holiday cheer to Shady Acres. Care to join us?"

"Love to!" said Carol. "Give me a minute to get my snow gear on!"

Amelia Bedelia smiled. With a real Carol coming along, they were officially caroling!

As the Holiday Elfers slogged through the snow, singing holiday songs, more and more people joined them. By the time they reached Shady Acres, it looked like the entire town was part of the Christmas caravan.

When Amelia Bedelia's mother went into Shady Acres to tell the residents that the holiday pageant had come to them, Amelia Bedelia spotted Dr. Wiggins in the crowd outdoors. Amelia Bedelia made her way over to her. Dr. Wiggins had Jack Frost on a leash, and he was wearing a Christmas sweater. As soon as Jack saw Amelia Bedelia, he jumped up and licked her face. Doc W grinned. "You'll never believe it," said the vet. "We got an anonymous donation, enough to buy a sweater for every dog. They looked so cute in them, we posted their photos on our website, and almost all the dogs got adopted!"

"Amazing!" said Amelia Bedelia, smiling. She bent down and gave Jack Frost a giant hug. "But no one adopted this cutie?"

Doc W smiled. "I did!"

Just then Amelia Bedelia's mother called her over to meet some of the residents of Shady Acres. Mrs. Diamond reached out and took Amelia Bedelia's mittened hand. "We were so sad when the pageant was canceled. Thank you for coming!"

"You're very welcome," said Amelia Bedelia.

"Hi, Amelia Bedelia," said a man with a big white mustache. "I'm Don Decker, and I'm so glad you're here. I love a good snow day. When I was young, my brother and sister and I made snow angels all over our front lawn." He smiled at the memory.

"Nice to meet you!" said Amelia Bedelia. She waved to Mrs. Diamond, Mr. Decker, and her mom and headed back to her friends for the sing-along.

Holly led the crowd as the Holiday Elfers sang every holiday song they knew, ending with "The Twelve Days of Christmas." The sun was bright, making the snow sparkle and glisten. Everyone was so happy just to be together.

"How could I forget this one? I sing this one every year," said Amelia Bedelia's mother. She jumped up and stood next to Holly. Together they led the crowd in singing "White Christmas."

Amelia Bedelia had an idea. She hopped on a wagon to share it with the group. "You got your wish, Mom," said Amelia Bedelia. "And Mr. Decker just reminded me of my favorite thing to do in the snow. Let's all make snow angels!

"If you don't know how, just watch me. First you drop in the snow like this!"

She flopped back in the snow. "Then you move your arms up and down and your legs in and out," she said, demonstrating. She stood up very slowly and carefully. "And look! An angel!"

Everyone cheered, then flopped back and got to work. Soon the lawn in front of Shady Acres was covered in snow angels.

Then the mayor stepped forward to make an announcement. "I want to thank you, Amelia Bedelia, and all the Holiday Elfers for bringing the spirit of the season to our town and for reminding us all how to have fun in the snow! No matter what age we are," he added, "it is truly wonderful to see you all here on this snowy day. What a terrific town we live in. What an amazing community we all are!"

The crowd clapped and cheered.

The mayor continued, "At our next city council meeting, I will propose that we make Christmas caroling and snow-angel making an annual event on the first snow day of the year!"

The crowd roared its approval.

When the cheers died down, Amelia Bedelia spoke up. "And now it's time for cookies!"

"And Pete's famous hot cocoa!" Pete called out, gesturing to the big urns he'd carried over from Pete's Diner.

Amelia Bedelia and her friends worked

hard delivering reindeer cookies and hot cocoa to everyone. It was fun to see so many familiar faces.

"Hello, Amelia Bedelia," said a voice she recognized. She turned around. It was Mr. Jack. He toasted her with his cup of hot cocoa. "Great job!" he said. He peered at her rosy face. "It looks like Jack Frost has been nipping at your nose."

"Oh no," said Amelia Bedelia. "He just likes to give slobbery kisses."

Snow Globe Encore

"Merry Christmas Eve!" said Amelia Bedelia as she made her way down the stairs. She and her parents had returned from the First Annual Outdoor Christmas Caroling and Snow-Angel-Making Event, their cheeks flushed and their spirits high. After changing into dry clothes, they had headed for the living room. Her mother was already curled up on the couch, gazing into the fire in the fireplace and admiring their Christmas tree. The lights gave everything a peaceful, soft glow.

"Oh, Mom," Amelia Bedelia said. "It's all so beautiful."

"Come sit down," said her mother, patting the cushion next to her. "You and your friends were wonderful today. I don't know how this day could be any better."

"It was really fun," said Amelia Bedelia. "Where's Daddy?"

"He went upstairs to get something," Amelia Bedelia's mother said. "He was being very mysterious."

Just then, her father came bounding

down the stairs. "You'll never believe this," he said. "But last week I was up in the attic looking for an extension cord, and I found this box hidden under the eaves." He handed it to his wife.

She opened it and gasped. "Our decorations!" she said. "Look, Amelia Bedelia!" She began pulling out candy canes, lollipops, and gingerbread men, all made of cardboard and decorated with glitter.

"They're so pretty!" said Amelia Bedelia. "Let's hang them on the tree."

When they were done, Amelia Bedelia's mother stepped back to admire their work. "How wonderful to have them again," she said. She sighed. "If only our snow globe had survived Uncle

Marvin. We could re-create our very first Christmas!"

Amelia Bedelia turned and raced upstairs. She came back down holding a wrapped gift. She had covered the box in dark blue paper and glued 3-D snowflakes all over it. She thought it was one of her very best designs.

"I don't want to open it—it's too beautiful!" said her mother.

"But that's the only way you're going to see what's inside," said Amelia Bedelia.

Her parents opened the box together. Her mom pulled out the gift, wrapped in tissue paper. She unwrapped it and gasped. "Oh, Amelia Bedelia," she said. "It's a snow globe!"

Amelia Bedelia's father turned on a lamp to get a better look. "Hey, it's got us inside!" He put his arm around his wife. "Just like the one Uncle Marvin broke. But this one is much better, because it has all three of us in it."

"And Finally too!" said Amelia Bedelia. "We started the Holiday Elfers so we could make money to buy Christmas gifts. Then I made enough money to buy a snow globe, but I couldn't find the perfect one in any of the stores in town. So, I decided to make it myself! It was easy, once I found the instructions."

"It's the best gift ever," said her father.

"Thank you, sweetie." Her mother wiped her eyes. "And thanks, Uncle Marvin."

"So you never spent your earnings," her father said. "You must have a pretty penny."

"More than one, Daddy. Hundreds and hundreds of them! But I donated them all."

"Donated? Where?" asked Amelia Bedelia's father.

"To the animal shelter. The dogs were cold and needed sweaters," said Amelia Bedelia.

Her mother laughed. "Amelia Bedelia, you never cease to amaze us. You are the gift that keeps on giving."

"Unfortunately, I am all out of presents," said Amelia Bedelia. "But how about a ho-ho-holiday hug?"

"You bet!" said her father, pulling them both in. "There's nothing like the holidays to make you realize the importance of holding your family close."

"Mmmmmmmmmmfffff," said Amelia Bedelia, her face pressed against his sweater.

"What did you say, cupcake?" asked her mother.

Amelia Bedelia leaned back. "I said, if I get any closer, I would be on the other side of you!"

Two Ways to Say It

I have a lot on my plate.

I have a lot of things to do.

We didn't have two pennies to rub together.

We were very poor.

Let's trim the tree.

Let's decorate it.

That's a wrap.

All done!

I'll be there with bells on.

I'm excited to join in.

Burn the candle at both ends.

Work very hard, day and night.

Crushed.

Very upset.

We're all ears.

We're listening carefully.

I'm tickled pink.

I'm very pleased.

Pool the money.

Share the money.

Make Your Own PHOTO

Supplies: glass jar with tight-fitting lid
baby oil
photo
clear packing tape
glitter
ribbon/small jewels/beads
(optional)

Tools: scissors
glue gun and hot glue (adult
supervision required)

Directions:

1. Set up a work area with newspapers,
paper plates, and paper towels. Remove any
labels from glass jar. (If there is glue stuck to
the jar, remove it by rubbing the jar with a
paper towel with baby oil
on it. Wash jar and make
sure it is completely
clean and dry.

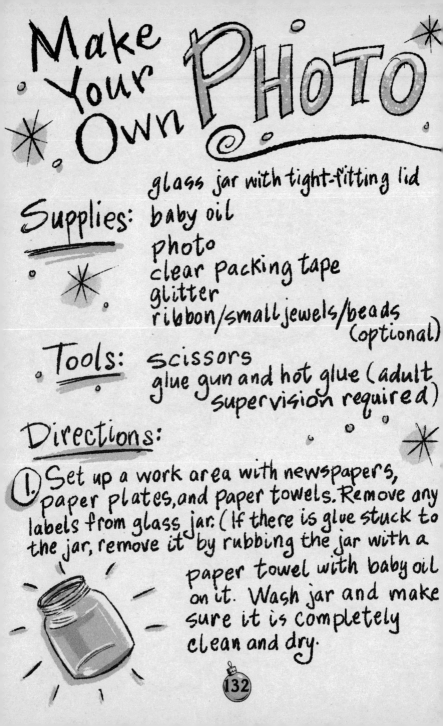

SNOW GLOBE

2. Select a photo that will fit on the inside of the jar lid, with room on the sides to screw the lid shut.

3. Trim photo with scissors.

4. Cover the photo with packing tape on both sides. Trim off the extra tape, leaving a thin border of tape around the photo. Press down firmly to make sure photo is sealed on all edges.

5. Ask an adult to help you with the glue gun. Apply a strip of hot glue to the center of the lid and place your photo on it. Allow glue to dry.

6. Working on a paper plate over newspaper, fill jar with baby oil. Pour glitter into the jar.

7. Tighten top and shake. How does it look? Do you have enough glitter? Once you are happy with the amount of glitter, it is time to seal your snow globe. ☺

8. Open jar and spread a thin layer of hot glue on the inside rim of the jar lid.

9. Replace lid quickly, before the glue dries, and screw it shut. Allow time for the glue to dry, then flip your snow globe over so it rests on the jar lid.

10. If you like, tie a ribbon around the base of the jar, or decorate your snow globe with jewels or beads.

SHAKE

whenever you want snow to fall on your favorite photo!

Amelia Bedelia's
Holiday Thumbprint Cookies

This recipe makes around 50 cookies!

Ingredients

3 sticks (24 tablespoons) of unsalted butter

¾ cup of granulated sugar

1 egg

½ teaspoon of vanilla extract

¾ cup of flour

jam (Amelia Bedelia likes strawberry jam,
but any kind of jam will work)

optional: chocolate chunks

1. Preheat oven to 350 degrees.

2. In a large mixing bowl, beat the butter and sugar together until smooth.

3. Add the egg and vanilla extract, and beat until completely combined.

4. Add the flour and continue beating, with your beater on low speed or with a wooden spoon, until the flour is just mixed in.

5. Shape the dough into small balls
   (about 2 tablespoons of dough each).

6. Place the balls on baking sheets,
   at least 3 inches apart.

7. Dip your thumb in water, and press the center
   of each ball, making a small indentation about
   an inch deep.

8. Place your jam into a glass bowl and heat it
   up until liquified (you can use a microwave).
   Then spoon about 1/2 teaspoon of jam into
   each thumbprint. You can also fill the
   thumbprints with chocolate if you prefer!

9. Bake until cookies are golden brown around
   edges, about 18 to 20 minutes.

10. Using a spatula, transfer the hot cookies to
    a wire rack, and let cool.

**Ask a grown-up for help with the oven
and microwave!**

The Amelia Bedelia Chapter Books

Amelia Bedelia wants a new bike—a brand-new, shiny, beautiful, fast bike. A bike like that is really expensive and will cost an arm and a leg!

Amelia Bedelia is getting a puppy—a sweet, adorable, loyal, friendly puppy!

Amelia Bedelia is hitting the road. Where is she going? It's a surprise!

Have you read them all?

Amelia Bedelia is going to build a zoo in her backyard. Better yet, she is going to invite all her friends to bring their pets and help plan the exhibits and rides.

Amelia Bedelia usually loves recess, but one day she doesn't get picked for a team and she begins to have second thoughts about sports.

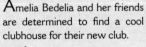

Amelia Bedelia and her friends are determined to find a cool clubhouse for their new club.

Amelia Bedelia is so excited to be spending her vacation at the beach! But one night, she sees her cousin sneaking out the window. Where is he going?

New steps inspire Amelia Bedelia and her dance school classmates to dance up a storm!

What does Amelia Bedelia want to be when she grows up? Turns out, the sky's the limit!

When disaster strikes and threatens to ruin her aunt's wedding, it's up to Amelia Bedelia to make sure Aunt Mary and Bob tie the knot!

An overnight camp is not Amelia Bedelia's idea of fun—especially not *this* camp, which sounds as though it's super boring and rustic. What Amelia Bedelia needs is a new plan, fast!

Amelia Bedelia and her parents are heading to the shore for summer vacation and that means sailing, surfing, eating a ton of ice cream, and just hanging out. And what about the mystery of the buried treasure?

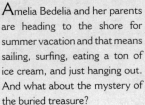

1

Amelia Bedelia and her friends celebrate their school's birthday.

2

Amelia Bedelia and her friends discover a stray kitten on the playground!

3

Amelia Bedelia and her friends take a school trip to the Middle Ages that is as different as knight and day.

Amelia Bedelia and her friends work to save Earth and beautify their town.

4

Mind your p's and q's
with Amelia Bedelia and her friends!

To save their annual ice cream party, Amelia Bedelia and her friends must learn (and practice!) a thing or two about manners, kindness, being polite, and being a good friend. But with Amelia Bedelia involved, there are guaranteed to be a few funny mix-ups along the way!

Coming
soon . . .

Amelia Bedelia is shaking like a leaf, scared stiff, and about to jump out of her own skin.
Sound silly?

You bet!

Get ready
to read

Amelia Bedelia
Scared Silly

coming just in time
for Halloween 2021!

BOO!

Amelia Bedelia

Scared Silly

BY HERMAN PARISH ♦ PICTURES BY LYNNE AVRIL